DETOUR: A Christian Novel

Christian Youth Faith-Walkers Series

C.Orville McLeish

Published by HCP Book Publishing, 2024.

DETOUR: A CHRISTIAN NOVEL

First edition. July 5, 2024.

ISBN: 979-8227236494

Written by C.Orville McLeish.

Also by C.Orville McLeish

Christian Youth Faith-Walkers Series
DETOUR: A Christian Novel

The Unshakable Series
FAITH: A Theological Memoir

Standalone
Girl Unknown
Who I Am In Christ Daily Devotionals
How to Receive Your Healing
Sons of God: A Study on the Biblical Narrative of the Sons of God
Made in God's Image: We are Partakers of God's Divine Nature

Watch for more at https://clevelandomcleish.com/.

To all the young people who stay with God, even when
the path gets difficult.

Chapter One

Caleb James was a preacher's kid. A "PK", in common vernacular. All his life he had been called a PK and he hated it. The life of a PK, in his mind, was dull and predictable. In a word, the PK life was lifeless.

As he sat watching his family eating yet another lifeless Sunday dinner, he decided that things would change real soon. No more eating the same roast chicken with fork and knife. No more listening to his mother's small talk.

And most important, no more listening to his father, Pastor Rudolph James, spout so-called wisdom from his seat at the head of the table. Caleb was 25 years old. If his brother John, older by 3 years, wanted to stay under the old man's thumb, then that was his business.

Caleb had had enough of doing his father's bidding. It was time to live life on his terms. His mother's voice cut into his private thoughts.

"Today was lovely, dear," Janet James said to her husband.

"Uhm," Rudolph mumbled in reply as he chewed a bite of chicken.

"I think the message was relevant," his mother said.

"No, it wasn't," Caleb interjected. "Dad was preaching about guineps and tofu. Why do all his messages have to have some reference to food?"

His mother gave him *the* look. "Caleb, please. Not today."

Caleb simmered down a bit. He knew what that look meant, and he wasn't in the mood for one of her lectures of being disrespectful to the message of God. So he decided not to push the issue on his father's sermon topics.

Caleb's brother John dabbed at the corners of his mouth with a cloth napkin. "I think it was a good message."

"You would think so you little zombie!" Caleb growled. "How about developing a mind of your own, big brother, instead of sopping up what everybody else thinks."

"Caleb!" his mother said, "You are way out of line."

Rudolph looked down his nose at his son. Caleb felt the heat from his stare. "I preach so people can understand and relate to what I'm saying," he shared. "The message was good, but did it accomplish anything, Janet?"

"I'm sure it did, honey. There were many who came to the altar."

"Yes, but not my son."

Rudolph James stared at his youngest son again.

Caleb rolled his eyes. "I'm gonna assume you are talking about me, so I will ask why would I need to go to the altar today? You preached about people being like guineps. Some can be stripped from the seed easily, while others take a little greater effort. How is that relevant to me?"

"Your attitude, for one."

"What's wrong with my attitude?"

"It's not Christ-like."

"Are you two really going to do this again today?" Janet asked.

Her husband went back to slicing his meat. "I'm just trying to have my dinner."

"I dream of the day the two of you get along," she said. "I don't even know what the problem is between you two."

"Conflict of interest maybe."

"How so, Pops?"

"I am interested in church, and you are not."

"Do you have any idea what it's like being a pastor's son?"

"Nope. My father mined coal and grew callaloo. He went to church twice. His wedding and his funeral."

"Well then, let me tell you what it is like being a pastor's kid, a PK, Pops. It feels like my own personal prison. No freedom. No space."

"Wherever the presence of God is ... there is liberty."

"There is no liberty in being your son. There are just rules, chains, curfews and padlocks. No fun. No freedom."

"Freedom to do what?"

Smiling, Caleb twirled his fork in the air. "Whatever I like."

"Then maybe you have outgrown this roof."

"Maybe I have."

There, he had said it out loud. His brother and mother stopped eating and stared at him, like he had just sprouted a third eye.

His father took a deep breath and leaned forward. "You are nothing but an ungrateful fool."

Caleb slammed his fist on the table.

Rudolph's nostril flared. His eyes grew large. "Did you just slam your fist on my table?"

Did the water in his glass just tremble?

"I apologize."

His father still looked like he was going to blow a blood vessel. "This house is mine, young man. All this furniture is mine. I am the one who took them out on hire purchase, and I am still paying for them. In this house, you own nothing; so, curtail that attitude, son."

Caleb got up from the table.

"I don't see why you can't be more like your brother?" His father mumbled over his cold dinner.

"Caleb please sit down and finish your dinner," Janet said. She looked like she was near tears.

"I've lost my appetite, mom. Excuse me."

Caleb left the table but even behind the closed doors of his room he could hear his parent's talking.

"I can't remember the last time Caleb finished eating his Sunday dinner," his father said.

"And, you have to stop comparing him to John," came Janet's reply. "You know he hates it."

"I can't help it. The boy gets under my skin."

Caleb rolled his eyes. *The feeling is mutual, Pops.*

"You can't fight fire with fire, my love."

"You shouldn't be taking his side, Janet. You saw what he did."

"I'm sure there was a reason."

"He walked out, five minutes into my message, and didn't come back till after I finished preaching. I think the reason is clear enough."

Janet got up from the table. "I will go see if Caleb is okay. Excuse me."

His mother went to Caleb's door and softly knocked, but he refused to answer it. After a few minutes, she left. Caleb kicked off his dress shoes and removed his necktie. He hated having to dress for Sunday dinner.

While he relaxed on his bed, he heard his father and big brother talking in the living room.

"You okay, son?" Rudolph asked John.

"Yes, sir."

John, always the proper one.

"You should go feed the pigs now, John, and then get some rest. You have work tomorrow."

"Yes, sir."

Caleb grinned. He hated feeding the pigs. So, his big brother was more than welcome to do that chore.

"And don't worry, John. We will be hiring someone to take care of the farm so you won't be so pressured."

The favorite son is always the oldest son.

"I appreciate it, sir," his brother said.

"Good, boy."

Treats him like the family pet. Just like a dog.

Caleb snickered as he stretched out on his bed. He knew he would never get the kind of treatment his brother got, because he would rather get caught dead than be his father's 'yes' man.

Feed the pigs. Sit up straight in church. Never be disagreeable.

More like never think for yourself.

Things were going to be different around here. Caleb would make sure about that. He planned on having a serious talk with his father. But first a quick nap.

An afternoon nap was the only good thing about Sunday, in Caleb's opinion.

He dropped off to sleep quickly, but his sleep was not restful. In fact, his sleep was plagued with a nightmarish vision of being in a dark room with high walls. Chains were wrapped around him. And he could find no way out.

A voice boomed over him. "He has buried me in a dark place, like a person long dead. He has walled me in, and I cannot escape. He has bound me in heavy chains. And, though I cry and shout, he shuts out my prayers. He has blocked my path with a high stone wall. He has twisted the road before me with many detours."

Caleb woke with a start. His heart was racing as he sat up. He recognized the words that the voice shouted. It was from the Bible. From his years of forced attendance in Bible College, he knew it was Lamentations 3:6-9.

I must break free.

Caleb struggled to his feet, drenched in sweat.

I must break free.

He unlocked his room door and walked slowly into the living room. His father was seated on the couch reading the Sunday paper.

"We need to talk sir, Pops."

His father looked over his glasses at Caleb and then at his watch.

"Talk time is at five thirty, son. I'm having a moment here."

"You're having a moment? Your son wants to talk to you, but you are busy having a moment. A moment! What, Pops! Do I make an appointment?"

Rudolph shook the folds from his paper. "That's how it usually works, son."

"Everything for you is a schedule. An appointment. I am your son. I think I should be able to talk to my father when I feel like it."

"There has to be some order or more so a structure to how we do things."

"Is there a book for that?"

"Parenting for Dummies."

Caleb raised an eyebrow. "You are taking advice from a book called Parenting for Dummies?"

"It's a good read and besides. It's just the way I ..."

"Like to run my house," Caleb interrupted. "I know that part."

His father stared at him. "So I will see you at five thirty."

Caleb crossed his arms and stayed put.

"Can you go find your own moment someplace else?"

"We need to talk, Pops."

"Talk about what?"

"This is the routine. On Sunday morning, you get up at five thirty and go to the bathroom. You do a number one at twenty-five to six, brush your teeth at twenty-three to six, do a number two at quarter to six then take a shower at six-thirty. Everybody in this house knows that at exactly a quarter to seven and not a second sooner the door to the bathroom will open and you will step out saying, 'Thank God for soap.' You will take a deep breath and disappear in your room to re-surface at seven thirty ready to leave for church."

"Yeah, so what's your point?"

"Then you and somebody will get into some argument because what you took one hour and fifteen minutes to do you expect three grown people to do in half an hour."

"I plan to put in an extra bathroom. You know that."

"The routine will still be the same."

"Why are you having so great an issue over what and how I do my thing?"

"In exactly three minutes you are going to look at your watch and say 'My God. Look at the time.' You will fold your newspaper neatly and tuck it under your arm as you rise out of that couch and head to your room saying 'Time for a nap.'"

"You think you have me all figured out, don't you?"

"It doesn't have to be like that, sir. You spoke about liberty, but true freedom is the ability to do what you feel like doing, whenever. I want to wake up at 5:30 Sunday morning and feel like I want to sleep a little late and just do it."

"The Bible says in the book of Proverbs ..."

"Can we leave the Bible out of this for once? I am sick and tired of hearing you quote scriptures that have absolutely no relevance to our line of argument."

Rudolph James put his paper down. "Excuse me!"

"I am sick and tired of a lot of things. I want out."

"Out of what?"

"I want out of this family."

"How do you get out of a family? I know you can have a sex-change, but you can't possibly have a blood change." His father chuckled.

"I can start by getting out of this house."

"Son, normally when children decide to run away, they don't really inform their parents."

"I'm not running away. I'm moving on. I need to live my own life."

"You should probably get a job first."

"Look, Pops, I know you have some money saved up that you intend to split between John and me when you expire. I am asking you for mine now."

"No way."

"You don't really love me, do you?"

"Of course, I do."

"Then say it."

"I don't have to, son," he said without taking an eye from his paper.

Caleb grunted. Sure, he said the words, but he didn't really mean it. "Just give me what you promised, so I can leave."

"Why are you doing this, son? You want me to just write you a check and let you go wander around in the wilderness, the same wilderness I spent all your life trying to make you avoid?"

Caleb hunched his shoulders. "Yes, a check would be nice."

"Son, God has a plan for your life. All you are doing right now is planning to take a detour."

The word "detour" gave him pause. The voice in his dream used that word.

Caleb shook it off. "It's mine to take, Pops."

"I guess you have made up your mind then?"

"Yes."

"Will we ever see you again?"

"Highly unlikely."

"Never forget where you came from, son."

"Right now, I am just concerned about where I'm going."

"Where is that?"

"Anywhere but here."

Caleb leaves the room without a backwards glance.

The clock in the living room struck 5:30 PM.

"My God! Look at the time," he heard his father exclaim. "Time to take a nap."

Time to get my own life.

Chapter Two

Another Sunday morning.

Caleb rolled out of bed slowly and allowed himself a good long stretch as he made his way to the door. He peeked out into the hallway outside his bedroom.

Just like every other Sunday in his life, he saw his brother John waiting by the closed bathroom door, reading a book.

Their mother joins John. She's wearing a bathrobe and has a large towel draped over her shoulders. "What time is it?"

John pulled a cell phone from his robe pocket. "Six forty-four."

"One minute more to ..."

Her husband stepped from the bathroom looking refreshed. "Thank God for soap." He inhaled deeply and walked past them.

Janet James looked confused. "Something is wrong."

John frowned back at her. "Yeah, I know. He came out one minute too soon."

"I know this thing with Caleb is killing him, but he refuses to talk about it."

"Is my brother really leaving?"

Caleb quickly pulled on his robe and joined them in the hallway.

"Seems so," his mother said. "John, you should go use the bathroom. You know your father will be out in ten minutes wondering why we are not ready for church."

"Ok mom," he said and slipped into the bathroom, closing the door behind him.

His mother greeted him with a smile. "Good morning, Caleb."

"Morning, mom."

"What is it with you and your father?"

"Ask him."

"I am asking you. You have a responsibility as a son to honor your father."

"You want to quote scriptures, mom? Here is one, 'Provoke not your children to wrath.'"

"Your father loves you."

"Yeah? He never shows it. Never says it. He spends all his time doing two things. Preaching and preparing his message."

"He provides for us as a father and a husband. Is there anything we have ever lacked?"

"Listen to what you are saying, mom. We do everything according to the book. If he gives me what is mine, I can provide for myself. I can't stay here mom, or I am going to lose my mind. I am like a bird with wings who has never been given the chance to fly."

"Not every bird with wings is supposed to fly."

"No use trying to talk me out of it."

"Are you going to church today?"

"It's highly unlikely."

"Your father will not be pleased."

"Is it even possible to please him?"

"You know your father lives the Bible to a tee. Train a child in the way he should go, and when he is old, he will not turn from it."

"He is over-righteous."

His mother shook her head. "Can you really be over-righteous?"

"We never go anywhere but church. Life has passed us by, mom. Look at you. When was the last time you guys went out on a date? When was the last time you danced? You were a dancer once. I have seen the pictures."

"Dancing took me to a place, once, that I never want to return to. To move forward sometimes, you have to leave some things behind."

"Well, I am not willing to do that."

"I know where you are, son. The road you are considering will take you to a very unpleasant place. You can either believe me, and forget taking this detour, or you can go ahead and find out for yourself."

Caleb saw the sadness in her eyes. "I guess I will be finding out for myself."

Any further conversation got cut short. At that moment, Rudolph stepped from his bedroom across the hall. He was fully dressed in his dark blue double-breasted suit.

"Why aren't you guys ready for church? Do we have to do this every Sunday?"

Janet James hugged Caleb, and gave him a sad smile before retreating into her bedroom.

Rudolph gave Caleb a questioning look. "That goes for you too, young man."

"I'm not going to church today."

"I don't seem to be hearing so well. It sounded like you said you are not going to church today."

"I did say that."

"Well, I assume that if you were sick, you would be in bed." The two men stood staring at each other for several seconds. His father spoke first. "Young man, go get ready for church."

"I'm not going."

"Devil, I rebuke you in the name of Jesus. Release my son. I declare deliverance now in the name of Jesus."

Caleb just folded his arms and looked away.

"Oh, so you are a stubborn demon. Huh?"

Rudolph removed his jacket and rolled up his sleeve. "No demon will have authority in my house. Caleb, my son, hang in there. Today is your day to be free."

Caleb steps back from his father. "I am not demon possessed."

His father grabbed Caleb's head with both hands. "Come out you lying stubborn demon. In the name of Jesus, come out! Hang in there, my son. This could get a bit rough."

Rudolph dragged him into the living room and threw Caleb down on the couch then started beating him with the Bible from the coffee table.

"In the name a Jesus," Rudolph yelled, "In the name a Jesus. In the name a Jesus ..."

"Ok...ok. I will go to church. Just get off me, please."

"Are you delivered, my son?"

"Yes, Pops. Whatever it was telling me not to go to church is definitely gone now."

"There is power in the name a Jesus."

Rudolph tucked in his shirt and donned his jacket again.

"Pops, I am still serious about leaving."

"Can we talk about this later?"

"I don't plan to be here later so we should talk about it now."

"Where is all this coming from, son?"

"All my life I have been living your dream. You wanted me to do a Bachelor's Degree in Theology. I did. You wanted me to take up Ministers Training, I did. But that's not me, Pops."

Rudolph looked dumbfounded. "I thought it's what you wanted."

"I did it because it's what *you* wanted."

"Why would you do it, because you think it's what I wanted you to do?"

Because I wanted your approval. That's what he wanted to say, but instead, he said, "I thought you wanted me to do it, so I did."

"Then what do you want?"

"That's what I hope to find out, but I can't do that here because I will always be seen as a pastor's son."

"I will not allow you to leave this house and go get yourself entangled with the world. I can't do it."

"This is my choice. I'm a man now."

"You are my son and as long as I am alive you will abide by my rules."

Caleb couldn't believe what he was hearing. "Then I wish you were dead!"

Rudolph looked like he was near tears. "You don't mean that."

"I don't want to be a part of this, Pops. You have held me back long enough and I do hate you for that. Its time I found my own way and I will do it with or without your blessing."

Caleb watched his father hang his head. His father's big hands opened and closed, but he did not look at his son in the eye. He did not say another word.

Caleb turned on his heels and left. He decided that he would go to one last church service and that was that. If his father had no more to say, then neither did he.

Chapter Three

Caleb shifts uncomfortably in the pew.

Another Sunday in church. Another Sunday sitting on these hard pews, listening to his father preach another sermon about food.

Big yawn.

"Praise the Lord, saints," Pastor Rudolph James exhorted. The people, with the exception of Caleb, responded with praise.

The pastor continued. "God has brought us through another week—and a challenging week it was—but we are here. Amen. Through the fire and through the flood God has seen us through. Anybody else in this house had a rough week?"

Caleb faked a yawn. Everyone else in the congregation responded affirmatively to their pastor.

"Amen," Rudolph went on talking as he slid his glasses on. "God has a word for us today. Praise the Lord. I'm gonna ask somebody to read for me from Psalms 1."

Oh no. Not Sister Florence.

Caleb rolled his eyes.

The elderly woman hobbled up to the podium beside the pulpit and opened the Bible. After what seemed like an eternity of flipped pages, she read loudly. "Blessed is the man."

"Blessed is the man," Pastor James repeated.

Then they took turns reading and repeating.

"Who does not walk in the counsel of the wicked?" she read.

"Who does not walk in the counsel of the wicked?" he repeated.

"Or stand in the way of sinners."

"Or stands in the way of sinners."

"Or sit in the seat of mockers."

"Or sit...are we getting this? Or sit in the seat of mockers."

"But his delight is in the law of the Lord."

"But his delight is in the law of the Lord."

"And on his law, he meditates day and night."

"And on his law ... some of us don't even read our Bibles. But God gives a promise to those who do. Pay attention now. Read on, my sister."

"He is like a tree planted by the streams of water."

"He is like a tree planted by the streams of water." Pastor James grunted like he was enjoying a juicy piece of fruit. "Uhm uhm!"

"Which yields its fruit in season."

"Which yields its fruit in season."

"And whose leaf does not wither."

Pastor Rudolph rocked back and forth on his heels. "Thank you, Sister Florence. David said thy word have I hid in my heart, that I will not go into sin against thee. When you put the word inside you. Amen. The Bible say, out of you will flow rivers of living water. I feel like preaching today."

He paused to drink some water then went on. "I think I'm gonna need more than water today. Can someone get me a red bull, please?"

He laughed. The congregation laughed. That is, everyone except Caleb laughed.

Here it comes, the food portion of the sermon.

Caleb tried to put his brain on autopilot. His father's loud sing-song preaching style, though, was very difficult to ignore, especially since he was sitting on the front row next to his mom and brother.

His father paused for another drink of water and dove back into his notes.

"I am thinking about Ackee," Pastor James said. "It grows on a tree that is planted in the ground. It bears in seasons. It can be poisonous but in due season, the Ackee is fit for consumption. Ackee is multi-dimensional. It has three sides. Some have two seeds and others have three. We are like the Ackee. The Bible says we will be like a tree planted by the rivers of water that brings forth fruit."

"Water is a source of life and sustenance for the tree. Without it, the tree would die and there would be no fruit. A tree that bears no fruit will be cast in the fire.

"I did some research on the Ackee tree, and this is what I found. Amen. Ackee is a fruit that grows on the Ackee tree. The Ackee tree grows to about 30 ft. high and bears bright red fruit. The fruit ripens to reveal pods of yellow edible Ackee, each with a black seed. Ackee is usually prepared with salt fish and onions. Bacon can be substituted for the salt fish. The flavor and texture is somewhat like scrambled eggs. Ackee is also the main ingredient in Jamaica's national dish. Ahh, I knew I wouldn't get an amen right there. Ackee is a national dish."

"We don't know who we are in God. We think we are ordinary people, but I am here to tell somebody today that we ain't ordinary. The Bible describes us as a peculiar people, a holy nation...a royal priesthood. God has called us out of darkness and into his marvelous light. We have reason to rejoice today. We face many challenges from day-to-day."

"The Bible says that in the last days many will fall to seducing spirits. We may think that we have time to take the long journey of self-discovery but judging by the signs of the times... the clock has stopped ticking. The hand has stopped moving and as a church, I want us to agree today on behalf of my son and others like him that God will help him to find his way back home."

Caleb felt his father's strong disapproval at that moment. They locked eyes and he saw a deep sadness there that he had never seen before.

Standing, he shook his head at his father standing in judgment over him behind the podium.

It was no better time to leave than now, he figured.

"Don't leave, son," his father said. Tears had started forming in his father's eyes.

"There's no help for me, Pops. I don't want to find my way back home. At least, not yet. When I'm ready. I'll come back home. But not now."

And with that declaration, Caleb turned his back on his father and left the church.

Chapter Four

Caleb James smiled. He was living the life. A pretty girl on his left. And a pretty girl on his right. And a tumbler of rum on the bar in front of him. Yes, he was living the good life he always wanted.

He downed his drink and the barkeep quickly refilled it.

Never empty.

"Ahh," he signed as he rolled the stiffness from his shoulders.

The good life!

One of the girls leaned in closer and whispered in his ear. "I need my money, CJ."

Oh how he liked the new nickname they'd given him. He reached for his wallet and gave her some cash. Her female working companion followed suit. He gave her some money too. After a kiss and a snuggle from each, he let them both leave him.

They'll be back, he assured himself.

A man approached him from across the bar. It was his new friend Bryan Singer. "Whaddup CJ?"

"Thank you for introducing me to those two sweet ladies, Bryan. King Solomon says it best. Eat, drink and enjoy the fruits of your labor."

"You should go easy, bro."

"One life to live. Isn't that what you always say? Live each day as if it's the last."

"Didn't know you buy it being all up in our faces with all that Jesus stuff."

"Let's leave the past where it belongs."

Bryan signaled the barista for a drink. When she comes, she also refilled Caleb's glass.

"This is my definition of liberty. I wake up when I feel like it. I drink when I feel like it and I can have any girl I want."

Bryan gave him a sly smile. "For the right price."

"Money answers all things," Caleb said, fanning a wad of bills.

"If the Bible is right about some things, wouldn't it be right about everything?"

"Why are you talking about the Bible? You have never showed any interest in what I used to say."

"Don't mean I don't go home and think about it."

"The Bible and everything it represents is just another level of oppression. It's just another means of enslaving the mind of the people. I am liberating myself from all that so if you want to talk to me. Talk to me about cars, money and girls. Nothing else matters to me right now."

Bryan shrugged. "I got my homeboy to line up a nice set of wheels for you."

"Now you talking my language."

"It's gonna cost you, Twenty Grand."

"Just tell me the time and the place. I also want a decent apartment in Jacks Hill where all the classy people live."

"What's wrong with the one I got you?"

"I am tired of it."

"You have only been there a month."

"That's two weeks too long man. I want to live like Solomon. I deny myself nothing my eyes desire; I refuse my heart no pleasure. My heart took delight in all my labor, and this was the reward for all my toil."

"You sure about that?"

"Yeah."

Bryan reached into his pocket and pulled out a bag with some white substance.

"What is that?" Caleb asked.

"If you want to go all the way, this is the thing that will take you there."

Caleb thought about it. Girls and fast cars was one thing. This was a horse of another color.

"What do you say, CJ? You wanna ride in the fast lane you gotta go with the flow. You gimme two grand for that bag and I guarantee you before you sniff the last drop, you and angels will be having a picnic on the same cloud."

Caleb took the bag and stared at it. "I have never done drugs."

"It's one, two, three, man. This stuff is user-friendly."

"I don't know about this man."

"Girls, fast cars, and drugs. It's society's trinity man. The perfect combination."

Caleb chewed on his lip. "Two grand?"

"Small price to pay for daily trips to heaven and beyond."

In the next instant, two policeman burst into the bar with guns drawn. "Police. Nobody move!"

Caleb is left holding the bag. Bryan Singer is nowhere to be found.

Chapter Five

Spending the night in a cold, dirty, smelly jail was not as bad as Caleb thought it would be. His father in the meeting room, his first visitor, on the other hand, was pure torture.

There was a small table with two chairs in the room Caleb was led to. One of the chairs was occupied by Rudolph James. Caleb reluctantly sits in the other chair opposite his father. A uniformed officer stood beside the door, keeping watch.

"What do you want, Pops?"

"It's nice to see you too, Caleb."

"I don't need a guilt trip or pity party from you."

"Not seeing you for a month is one thing. Getting a call that you are in jail. That's something else. Getting the call from someone other than you," he said and indicated the officer standing by the door. "Now, that's disappointing. Is this what you wanted?"

"It feels better to be in jail than in the same house with you."

"You don't mean that. Look son, I know you are angry and maybe even bitter, but that doesn't justify you making poor choices."

"At least, they are my choices totally independent of other influences."

"Why do you hate me so much?"

"You always said God hated sin, but loved the sinner. I don't hate you, Pops, but I do hate your ways. It was never easy being your son and abiding by all your rules and way of life."

"I tried to raise you the best way I know how."

"What are you doing here, Pops?"

"I came to make your bail."

"Why?"

"You're my son and I care about you."

"You say the words, but I don't think you mean them. How could three little words be so empty?"

"I want you to come home, Caleb."

"Did you know that when someone get arrested, they are entitled to one phone call?"

"Yes."

"Don't you think it strange, that you are not the one I called?"

"I know we have our differences."

"No, Pops. Not differences. Between you and me it's far more than a difference of opinion and you were right about one thing. I lost interest in church."

"Have you thought about where you are coming from and where you are now?"

"Every day."

"And you choose this lifestyle?"

"Every single hour of every single day."

"You spent the night in jail."

"Just a small pit stop in the journey."

"The god of this world has blinded you, my son."

"Even so, I am having the time of my life; I don't need you or God."

Bryan entered with one of the women from the bar.

"It's about time you got here," Caleb said to Bryan. He leaned over and kissed the woman on the lips. "Hi, Celeste."

Rudolph looked away.

"Pops, meet my girl Celeste and my best man Bryan. Guys, this is my Pops."

Celeste waved at him as Bryan shook his hand.

"CJ talks about you all the time," Bryan said.

"Really?"

Bryan let out a hearty laugh. "Naw. He never mentions you. Anyway, boys and girl, we gotta go. Caleb, you are a free man."

Caleb follows them to the door and whispered to his friend. "How did you manage to spring me out of jail, bro? They caught me holding the bag."

"As you said, money answers all. I bought your freedom, so you owe me 30 grand. Let's bounce. We got things to discuss."

As Bryan and Celeste leave, Caleb turned one last time to his father. "I have friends in high places, Pops. I'm sorry you wasted the trip."

"My son, if you forget everything I taught you, don't forget this one thing, everybody needs God."

"Yeah, whatever."

Caleb left his dad standing alone, but heard him calling to him. "What else can a father do for his son but commit him to You, Lord. May he find You, in all this mess, before it's too late."

Chapter Six

Caleb woke up alone with a huge hangover. He rubbed his head and looked around, trying to remember the events of the night before.

His surroundings are familiar. He's in one of the private party rooms of their favorite night club. But he can't remember coming here in the first place.

Smells of cigar smoke and whiskey linger in the air.

"Celeste?" he called out.

No answer.

He tried again. "Bryan?"

No answer.

"Where are you guys? God, my head hurts."

He tried to get up but fell back on the couch.

The club owner entered carrying a small silver tray. The tray held a receipt and a credit card.

"Where is everybody?" Caleb asked the owner.

"They left a few hours ago."

"They wouldn't leave without me."

"They did."

"Why?"

"That's a question for them. My only concern is you settling this bill."

He looked down at the credit card on the tray. "You have my credit card."

"I tried it twice. It declined."

"What about my debit card?"

"Insufficient funds."

"No way!

Caleb took the receipt and looked at it. The amount took his breath away. "Are you kidding me? I owe you four hundred grand?"

"Got news for you, buddy, you also owe for credit you have made over the past five months here in this club as well as rent for my place up in Jacks Hill."

"You are my landlord?"

"Yep. The name is Ralph. And as much as I am enjoying this conversation, I only want you to settle this bill and leave."

Ralph?

"I've never met you. Hold on a sec! Are you telling me I haven't been paying my bills?"

"Well, sir, the books cannot lie, and the books say you owe."

"Bryan had access to all my accounts, and he has been paying my bills."

"Bryan and your other *friends* left and said you would take care of it. I need to settle this today, so you need to tell me if we are gonna do this the easy way or the hard way."

"How could they do this to me?"

"If there is one thing I have learnt in this business it's that money has no friends and shows no favoritism. What you need to do is tell me how you plan to settle this bill if you have no money."

"I don't know."

"Well, you can't leave here until this bill is settled. Don't you have someone you can call?"

After a long pause, "No."

Ralph sat down. "Well, can't say I haven't seen this before."

"Seen what?"

"The story of the prodigal son. You would think that after 2000 years since the story was first told, you young people would learn."

"I don't know what you are talking about."

"I know you, son. I have been to your father's church. I have seen you sing on the choir and was more than disappointed to see you here. What you had is what everybody needs and you left it all behind."

Caleb looked away. "You don't know me."

"Maybe not that well, but I know the road you are on and believe it or not...whoever you are and, however different you might think you are from everybody else...this road takes you to the same place."

"If you are so knowledgeable of right and wrong, why are you here?"

"Because I'm a fool in love with money who is too weak to walk away from it. But I do have respect for the church and people like your father and know that's where I should or need to be. I would like to think that I am on the road to God, and occasionally I pass people like you going the opposite way and I do wonder."

"What do I do now then, Wise Ralph?"

"You are going to start paying your debt."

"How?"

"Normally, I would file charges and let you spend time in prison, but because of who your father is, I will be a little more lenient. I'm giving you a job."

"A job? In this club."

"Not exactly. I'm a businessman, see. I have lots of businesses." Ralph pulled out a brochure and spread it out in front of Caleb.

Happy Acres Farm were the big words across the top of the paper. Pictures of happy pigs danced along the border.

Ralph was all smiles. "I have a pig farm and I need help."

"I don't think so."

"It's your choice, kid."

"If I agree to work on the pig farm, how would that work?"

"I pay ten dollars an hour, so if you work 24 hours your debt should be settled in four and a half years."

Caleb's mouth dropped open. "Four and a half years?"

Ralph nodded. "Your choices either make you, or break you, son. There is no such thing as a free ride. Get up. Let's take a little trip to my farm."

The trip to Happy Acres Farm was not a happy one for Caleb. Ralph spent the day with him and showed him the ropes and left him on his own.

The slop-filled days turned into slop-filled weeks. The weeks into years. Through summer, fall, winter, and spring, he cared for the pigs. He often thought about his family and about the wildlife that got him a one-way ticket to the farm.

Through every kind of storm you could imagine, Caleb was there tending to the pigs, making sure they were well-fed and safe from harm. One day, a fiery storm came out of nowhere. There was a violent clap of thunder and the brightest flash of lightning he ever saw. It scared him nearly to death. And, it also brought him to his senses. Suddenly he realized that he had been on the farm for more than his allotted time.

He decided to pay Ralph a visit.

On his way to find his boss, Caleb met Bryan and Celeste in the club. They were having drinks and laughing at each other's jokes.

Confused, they looked at a ragged and dirty Caleb and they turned up their noses.

"Do I know you, man?" Bryan asked. "Celeste, you got any change to give this ragged freak?"

"No change, sugar."

Caleb pounded their table. "I have been living like this for five years. No home. No friends. No money."

"That's sad man."

"Is that all you have to say?" His anger was growing.

"I don't see what that has to do with me."

Caleb grabbed Bryan by the collar. Bryan pulled out a knife and Caleb eased off.

"Easy, fool. You getting my silk dirty."

"I thought you were my friends."

"If friends are people who take you for what you got, then we were friends."

"So now you know me?"

"Honestly did not recognize you at first, bro. You look different. Smell different too. Is that pig poo I smell?"

"How could you do this?"

"This was your choice, bro. Not mine. You wanted to live life in the fast lane. That don't come cheap."

"You pretended to be my friends."

"In my world the word 'friend' is relative."

Celeste leaned forward and placed a hand over Caleb's arm. "You should go home, Caleb. You don't belong here."

"Home? I have been eating pig food for five years. I can't tell the last time I had a bath, and you are talking to me about home. My home is with pigs."

"Your home is where your heart is," she cooed. What sense did that make? Was she high?

"I thought you loved me, Celeste?"

"Maybe I don't know what love is."

"You know, I don't think the boss-man would appreciate you being in his club like this. Bad public relations."

"The world is round, Bryan. What goes around usually comes right back around."

"You shoulda thought about that before you hooked up with us."

"I wonder if you could bring yourself to say it," Celeste interjected.

"Say what?"

"That your father was right."

Caleb felt like he had been punched in the stomach.

"As much as I am enjoying this little reunion, we got some business on the road to take care of. Soooo, see you, pal."

Bryan pulled Celeste up from her chair and together they staggered toward the door. Caleb glanced around the packed club. He pushed people aside as he made his way to the bar. Maybe the barista would know where Ralph was.

He got dirty looks from everyone. He didn't care. He wasn't going to leave without talking to Ralph.

"Ralph," Caleb called out when he reached the bar.

The barista was standing far away with her hand over her nose.

Ralph came out of the back room. "Why are you in here? You are chasing away my customers. You should go."

"I feed the pigs, remember?"

"No. I mean you should go home."

"I don't understand."

"You have paid your debt in full with a little extra."

Ralph took some bills from his wallet and handed them to Caleb. "That should be enough to get you a decent bath and a cab trip home."

"I'm free?"

He could barely believe it.

"Please go home."

"I can't."

"Why not?"

"They will never accept me back as their son."

"You might not have to worry about that."

"Why?"

"That storm we had earlier was no ordinary storm. The world has changed. Go home. I think you'll understand what I mean when you get there. You will just have to see it for yourself."

Ralph hung his head and left Caleb standing bewildered at the bar.

A million questions flooded Caleb's mind. He figured he would find out soon enough. With the money Ralph gave him, he was able to check into a nice hotel and get a nice haircut and shave. He bought himself some new clothes and shoes.

He felt like a new man, but he noticed something strange about his town. It had changed in some major ways. People everywhere were talking about the 'Big Storm that changed everything.'

He didn't know what all of that was about. All he knew was he had to make it home. When he finally walked through the door, he found the house empty.

On the dining room, he found three plates of half-eaten food. And in each of the three chairs, he saw three separate piles of clothing. It was as if his father, mother, and brother had stripped in the middle of dinner, left their clothes, and walked out naked.

This is totally weird.

Caleb ran through the house. "Pops, where are you."

No answer.

"Mom!" he called out frantically.

He heard a familiar voice. "They are not here," the woman's voice said.

But it wasn't his mother's voice. It was the voice of Sister Florence.

"Sister Florence?"

She laughed. "Sister? Now that's funny."

"What are you doing here?"

"I wouldn't be here, if I was really a Sister of Christ."

"What's going on? Where is my family?"

"They are gone."

"Gone where? Did they move? Why would their clothes still be here?"

"You ask a lot of questions. Didn't you hear about the Big Storm?"

"Yes, I've heard talk about it but what's that got to do with anything?"

"There is nobody here but me and you."

"My father loved this house. He would not leave just like that."

"He did leave. He went to a better house."

"Where?"

"Where the streets are made of gold and there are no tears."

Caleb got an uneasy feeling in his stomach. "Are they dead?"

"No son. They were taken up. Raptured."

Raptured?!

Sister Florence reached for her Bible and read from one of the gospels, "But as the days of Noah were, so shall also the coming of the Son of man be. For as in the days that were before the flood they were eating and drinking, marrying and giving in marriage, until the day that Noah entered into the ark, and knew not until the flood came, and took them all away; so shall also the coming of the Son of man be. Then shall two be in the field; the one shall be taken, and the other left. Two women shall be grinding at the mill; the one shall be taken, and the other left. Watch therefore: for ye know not what hour your Lord doth come."

Caleb knew the passage in Matthew 24, but he could not believe his ears. "What are you saying? They can't really be gone. That was just a story in the Bible."

"No, Caleb. It wasn't just a Bible story. They are really gone. We are the ones who were left."

Caleb's knees grew weak. He sat down in one of the dining room chairs.

"The Rapture." The words sounded strange coming from his lips.

"The TV news said that millions of people just disappeared off the face of the earth."

"This can't be happening."

"I found this letter by the door. It's from your father to you."

Caleb took the letter and opened it. "My son. I miss you. I look for you to return to me every single day. It's hard to believe that four years have gone since you left. The last time I saw you things never quite panned out the way I had hoped and there was much that went unsaid. I am sorry. So much has changed in four years, and I have had to face myself and the choices I made over the years. I just wanted you to know that *I love you.* It's so easy to write and I never quite understood why it was so hard to say with feeling; but I have been practicing and when I see you again, I will be able to say it. My father never told me...but I will tell you. We have a lot of catching up to do Caleb and you will be glad to know that...wait, I just heard a sound. It sounded like a trumpet..."

Caleb dropped the letter on the floor. This was unbelievable.

"Not quite the way you thought it would have worked out?" Sister Florence said. "No fatted calf. No party to welcome you, prodigal son, back home."

"Why are you here? You were an active member of the church, serving on many committees and singing on the choir. Why were you left behind?"

"I knew about Jesus Christ from what I read and what other people told me, but I never met Him. I only prayed and read my Bible when I went to church, but there was no relationship. I never fully surrendered myself to Him because I still wanted to do my own thing."

"You were a hypocrite?"

"We are all hypocrites at some point or another. Pretending to be someone we are not. It's human nature."

"Keep telling yourself that."

"The thing is, everything I thought mattered means absolutely nothing now. I would have given it all up to be called a friend of God."

"We all have regrets."

"But now we know the truth."

"Now is too late."

Sister Florence sat down beside Caleb and hugged him. In that moment, he realized that he was in a world where all its carnal pleasures were never meant to last. He knew that eternity was forever and there was only one of two places to spend eternity.

He finally understood that Jesus was real and that his fleshly choice to squander his life on sinful living had cost him eternity with God.

With bitter tears, Caleb James realized that he was the Prodigal Son who did not make it back home in time. He had taken a terrible detour, but he had realized that too late.

Personal Reflection

Journaling and personal reflection are very good practices to develop early in life. These stories weren't written just to entertain but to provoke thought and introspection, with the hope of helping readers make better choices in life and walk by faith. Get a journal and answer these questions as you reflect on the story you just read.

1. If you had a father like Rudolph, would that have an impact on how you saw yourself and the church?
2. Do you agree with Caleb that life in the world is more fun than life in church?
3. Do you agree that bad company corrupts good character? Explain why from your own personal experience.
4. How important is it to have good influences in your life as a youth growing up?
5. Do you agree with Sis Florence that we are all hypocrites? At times, pretending to be someone we are not?
6. What key lesson did you learn from this story?

Preview Chapter from the Next Book in the Series

Chapter 1

"The wages of sin is death! All you sinners need to repent! God is going to burn this city like Sodom and Gomorrah, and you all will die!"

The words rang out loudly and blended with the music that blasted from Sammy's Liquor Store. On the steps leading from the store sat Gomer and Celeste, looking on the man that was proclaiming their supposed death. To the world they were considered ladies of the night, in other words they were prostitutes. In their own eyes they were merely making a living, and doing it in the best way that they knew how. Gomer nudged her friend with her elbow, and rolled her eyes dramatically as they looked at the man. His words had little meaning to them, but it was great amusement to see him in action with his Bible swinging as he spoke. Gomer toyed with the bottle, and took a huge swig from it, while watching the man.

"God hates sinners! Especially prostitutes! You will die in your sins! Repent! Repent! Repent! All who want Jesus, come to this altar now."

Even though the man spoke loud, he did so with no passion. The only thing that was clear was the contempt he felt for his audience. "Come to the altar! This is your chance!" he demanded, but nobody responded. "Come on!" he said one more time, and then with resignation, clearly evident in his voice, he said. "May God have mercy on you!"

He closed his Bible, and walked off with his head held high, thinking that they would be doomed anyway. He felt that he'd done all that God required of him.

"Idiot!" Gomer said as they watched him go.

"Ah hate him. Sending everybody to hell. He's probably sinning more than we," Celeste said with a dry laugh and Gomer smiled.

"Only difference between him and me is that me drink me rum and do my thing in public." To prove her words to be true, Gomer lifted the bottle to her mouth and gulped some of it down.

Celeste clicked her tongue and said, "As if they're any better than we."

They kept their gazes on the man and watched how he went on his knees. The man lifted his hands to the sky as if he was saying an earnest prayer.

A snicker could be heard from Celeste, and she said, "Let him preach! Nobody listens. Maybe he'll do better with God listening." They burst out laughing at the man who eventually got up and walked off.

"Here's to those who aren't hiding behind some hypocritical mask!" Gomer said and lifted the bottle up high as if to formalize her words with a salute. The bottle then went straight to her mouth and she drank.

"You need to stop drinking that stuff," Celeste chided, but Gomer just laughed some more.

"You, my dear friend, need to start. I don't know how you don't drink in this line of work."

The mood changed instantly and Celeste gave Gomer a sideways look before saying gravely, "Drinking killed my mother."

Gomer looked down. She knew that about Celeste's mother already. No disrespect was meant, but she also didn't want to be compared to a dead woman. She put the bottle down next to her and said, "Alright! Alright, fine! No sob story. Okay!"

While she spoke, Celeste looked off in the distance and saw a familiar face. "Hey, ah see one of your customers."

Gomer looked up to see one of her customers approach. He was a good paying customer too, and she smiled seductively.

"Looks like Carlos. Sweet! I need a new iPhone and iPad," she said and sat up a little straighter.

Celeste laughed. Those were the type of customers they wanted. The ones who made everything worth their while. "Go do your thing," she told Gomer, but her friend grabbed the bottle with one hand and Celeste's hand with the other. She pulled Celeste up with her and said, "Not leaving you!"

They both giggled and laced their arms together as they walked to Carlos.

Hosea paced back and forth. His day had gone well and he was able to tick some things off his to-do list. The most important one was that he had to go out and spread the news of God wanting people to repent. Nobody repented, but his work was doing his part. It was like taking a horse to the water, but he would not be able to force it to drink. Same with those street people, he thought. He could tell them that they'd go to hell, and that God will destroy them, but he could not force them to stop being hard-headed. It felt good to know that he had done his part. Hosea smiled, but he also knew that he was not done with the list. He needed to talk to God. He had a serious request. As he paced the width of his room, Hosea took a deep breath. God knew his heart, and he was convinced that God would take him seriously. He grimaced. At least he hoped that God would see his request as serious enough to be granted. This was it, he thought. He walked to the side of his bed and kneeled down.

"God," he started with closed eyes, "I wish you would just talk to me like how you talk to Moses. I know you're not a respecter of persons and I know you hear me when I pray."

Hosea paused. For a moment he thought about ways to state his case, when he heard a voice say, "Hosea!"

Strange, he thought, he knew that he was alone in the house. Hosea hesitantly opened one eye and looked around.

Was he mistaken, he wondered. "Who said that?" he asked and opened his other eye, just in case he missed something the first time. He saw no one.

Hosea closed his eyes again and rubbed his hand over his face. It was important to be lucid, he thought, and then he asked, "God? Was that you?"

"My sheep know my voice." The words reverberated through the room and this time Hosea's eyes flew open.

"Whoa! God, this is, whoa! This is awesome," Hosea said while still looking around to see if God was there in a physical form. Speaking to himself, he said out loud, "First time that I'm hearing your voice so clear." Then, he directed his speech to God, "I can finally hear you, God. This is amazing."

"Hosea, this place has become as vile as Sodom."

Hosea nodded. Yes, he was in full agreement. There was a problem, and he knew God would take care of it. He knew exactly what happened to Sodom, and he was glad God was discussing it with him. He would have enough time to get away before the fire came down to destroy the place. Thinking quickly, Hosea said, "God, I just need two days. Me and Pops will leave and you can just destroy everybody else."

He was not prepared for the next thing he heard, "You want me to kill the people I love and died for?"

A deep frown revealed his confusion, and Hosea answered, "Well, yes, that's what you did to Sodom, right?"

"So, I should spare you and kill them?"

Hosea wanted to shout the words, 'of course', but instead he said as calmly as he could, "Sounds like a good idea to me."

"I love them as much as I love you, Hosea. If I kill them, I would have to kill you."

This time, Hosea was sure that he didn't hear correctly. It didn't make sense at all, he thought. Needing some clarity, he asked God, "Why should the righteous die with the sinners?"

"It's simple, Hosea," God stated, "you told your father yesterday that you loved his cooking. Is that true?"

"He's old! I don't want to hurt his feelings."

"That makes you a liar."

The words sunk in, but it wasn't very welcome. Slowly, Hosea got up from his knees and sat on the bed. After a long time thinking, he responded, "I get your point."

"No, you don't. Hosea, your preaching has no effect because it lacks something. You don't love them."

"Love? God, these are prostitutes selling their bodies literally outside my door, and you want me to love them?" Hosea said, hoping above hope that God would see it his way. Surely God would understand, he thought. He continued to say, "Did you know there are people who prefer to kill me than listen to your word? And you want me to love them?"

"Sin is sin. You should not judge another man. Like them, you are also a sinner Hosea."

"God, no, I am a Prophet. A righteous man!"

"Hosea, Hosea, there is only one who is righteous. He shed his blood for you. He shed it for them too. I saved you, Hosea, and I want to save them."

Hosea shook his head and looked out of his window. He never liked what he saw outside. It was a sick world. No, it was a dying world. They never listened when he told them to repent. They were a hopeless bunch of people. "God, don't you see that you're wasting your time with them?" He knew that God was omniscient, but he wished that it was possible to convince God of what was really out there.

"You lack understanding, Hosea. That is why you preach hate and condemnation. You go without being sent. You will not preach another message until you understand my love for sinners."

He closed his eyes briefly, as God spoke, and slowly opened them. "Okay, Lord, what do you want me to do?" he asked submissively.

"I want you to get married."

It was an idea with lots of merit, and Hosea smiled. Getting married was not a hard task, and God obviously wanted him to further enjoy the life he had, Hosea thought.

"Well, that sounds good, God. Of course, I'll do it."

"I am giving you a wife. Her name is Gomer." God said.

Hosea marveled at the statement.

"Where do I find Gomer?" he asked after a while.

"She will find you, tomorrow. She will be wearing a red skirt with a matching striped top."

Hosea nodded obediently and said with his chest pushed out, "Red is my favorite color. Niiiiice. Sounds like a wealthy girl. Very ambitious and independent, she must be. God, I am ready."

Hosea thought about it for a moment, and then asked, "So, God, seeing that you talk to me like Moses, can I see you too?"

"You will see me when you die!" came the response.

It was another response that he didn't expect. "That's harsh," he protested. His words were met with silence.

"God?"

Still nothing.

"God!"

No response came. Hosea waited a while, and then said softly, "Finally, I get a wife. This must be a special girl. Exceptional. One of a kind." He thought about the girl, and whispered, "Gomer..." He liked the way her name rolled off his tongue. Yes, Gomer will be a great wife for him.

Don't miss out!

Visit the website below and you can sign up to receive emails whenever C.Orville McLeish publishes a new book. There's no charge and no obligation.

https://books2read.com/r/B-A-GABRB-SIXPD

BOOKS 2 READ

Connecting independent readers to independent writers.

Did you love *DETOUR: A Christian Novel*? Then you should read *Girl Unknown*[1] by C.Orville McLeish!

★★★★★ "It's been a long time since I couldn't put a book down. This is one I will think about for a long time." - Amazon Reviewer

Meet Chloe Cleopatra Taylor, a young woman whose haunted past casts a dark shadow over her present. Her life is filled with relentless challenges—balancing her career, navigating her mother's battle with addiction, and seeking her place in the world—Chloe's path takes an unexpected turn when unexplainable events begin to unfold around her.Soon, the

---

1. https://books2read.com/u/311zEW

2. https://books2read.com/u/311zEW

boundary between reality and the ethereal blur, and Chloe finds herself in a world where dreams and truths intertwine. Memories once forgotten surge to the surface from the depths of her mind, and she needs answers. In her pursuit of answers, Chloe is driven to peel away the layers of her father's history, setting off a chain reaction that will shatter the very foundation of her existence.Her father's death is a mystery that threatens everything Chloe cherishes. Her world is thrust into chaos as she confronts her inner demons and the truths she has long avoided. She discovers a connection between her and her mother that defies comprehension. The deeper she digs, the more mysterious her journey becomes threatening the very world she has created for herself. Chloe is gifted and poised to change the world, but her journey will reveal a truth about her that may take it all away.

Read more at https://clevelandomcleish.com/.

Also by C.Orville McLeish

Christian Youth Faith-Walkers Series
DETOUR: A Christian Novel

The Unshakable Series
FAITH: A Theological Memoir

Standalone
Girl Unknown
Who I Am In Christ Daily Devotionals
How to Receive Your Healing
Sons of God:A Study on the Biblical Narrative of the Sons of
God
Made in God's Image: We are Partakers of God's Divine Nature

Watch for more at https://clevelandomcleish.com/.

About the Author

C. Orville McLeish is a successful entrepreneur, and an acclaimed multi-award-winning author, playwright, and screenwriter. He is a professional ghostwriter, copy editor and self-publishing service provider. With a deep commitment to intellectual and mystical theology, he intertwines his passion for health, fitness, longevity, and Christian spirituality. A proud graduate of Writer's Digest University and the School of Kingdom Ministries, Cleveland is currently pursuing a master's in theological studies at Gordon-Conwell Theological Seminary. Read more at https://clevelandomcleish.com/.

www.ingramcontent.com/pod-product-compliance
Lightning Source LLC
Chambersburg PA
CBHW071510130726
47997CB00006B/2478